This Little Tiger book belongs to:

_____

_____

_____

To Donna, a winter's child, with love
~ K W

For my cousin Grace
~ A E

LITTLE TIGER PRESS LTD,
an imprint of the Little Tiger Group,
1 Coda Studios, 189 Munster Road,
London SW6 6AW
www.littletiger.co.uk

First published in Great Britain 2011
This edition published in 2016

A CIP catalogue record for this book is
available from the British Library

When Will It Snow?

Kathryn White • Alison Edgson

LITTLE TIGER

LONDON

"Winter is coming, Little Bear," Mother Bear said. "Soon, icy winds will blow, bringing the soft, white snow. We must snuggle down to sleep, safe in our den."

"I don't want to sleep," said Little Bear. "I want to play in the snow!"

Then he bounded away to hide.

"Oooh, I love hide-and-seek!" cried
Squirrel, peeping down from a tree.
"Sshhh!" Little Bear hushed.
"I'm not playing hide-and-seek.
I've run away."

Mole popped up from his burrow with a "Boo!"

So Little Bear stamped his foot, "I'm not playing, I'm hiding!"

"Why's that?" asked Squirrel.

"Because if I go home, I'll have to sleep for the whole winter. And I'll *never* know what snow is like."

"I'll show you what snow's like," chuckled Squirrel. "It just falls from the sky, like this." And she tossed some acorns into the air.

"Snow doesn't bounce like that!" cried Mole. "Snow is soft and wet – like this!"

He wiggled his bottom and dived into a puddle. *Sploosh!* Little Bear squealed with delight.

"Snow is thick," said Squirrel. "You can make snowmen with it and . . . SNOWBALLS!" And she tossed a ball of mud towards her friend.

Little Bear ducked but . . .

Splodge! The mud-ball soaked poor Mole!

"Snow is brilliant!" laughed Bear.
Suddenly there were mud-balls
flying everywhere.

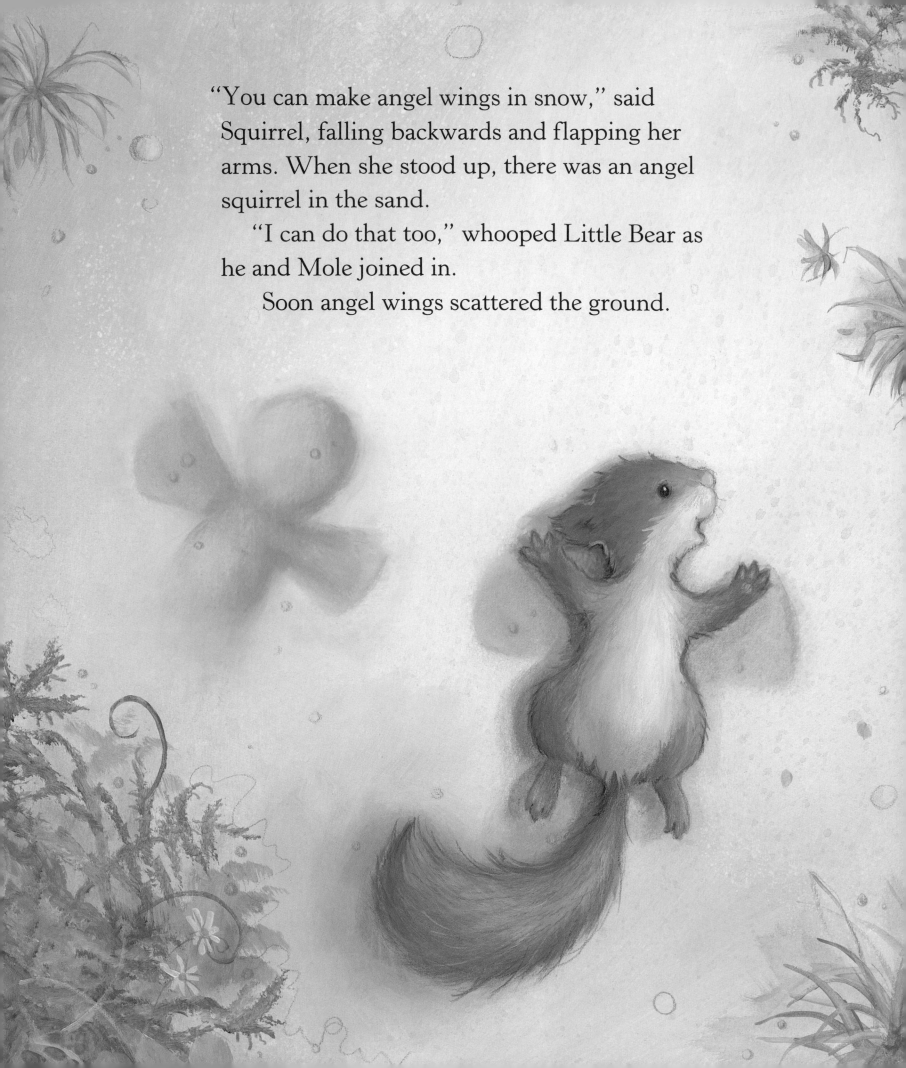

"You can make angel wings in snow," said Squirrel, falling backwards and flapping her arms. When she stood up, there was an angel squirrel in the sand.

"I can do that too," whooped Little Bear as he and Mole joined in.

Soon angel wings scattered the ground.

Bear looked at his friends. "Will you two
play in the snow while I'm asleep?"
he asked.
    "Oh yeah!" said Mole.
"Hide-and-seek is great
in the snow."

Just then, Little Bear heard his mother calling.
He flopped down in a huff.

"Grouchy grizzly!" giggled Mole, making
him a funny hat.

"Don't forget me," said Bear.

"'Course not!" said Squirrel.

But as Bear turned to take one last look at his friends, they were already playing without him.

"Us bears sleep through the winter," said Mother Bear softly. "And when we wake, the cold snow is gone."

"Will my friends be gone too?" whispered Little Bear.

"True friends are always there for you when you wake, like the blossom on the trees and the warm sunshine."

Then Mother Bear snuggled her little one gently into bed.

When Little Bear trudged back into his cave, Mother Bear reached out for a hug.

"I don't want hugs," said Bear. "I want to see the snow."

Bear ran straight to the muddy puddle to look for Squirrel and Mole. But they were nowhere to be seen.

"They've gone," he sighed. "They've forgotten all about me."

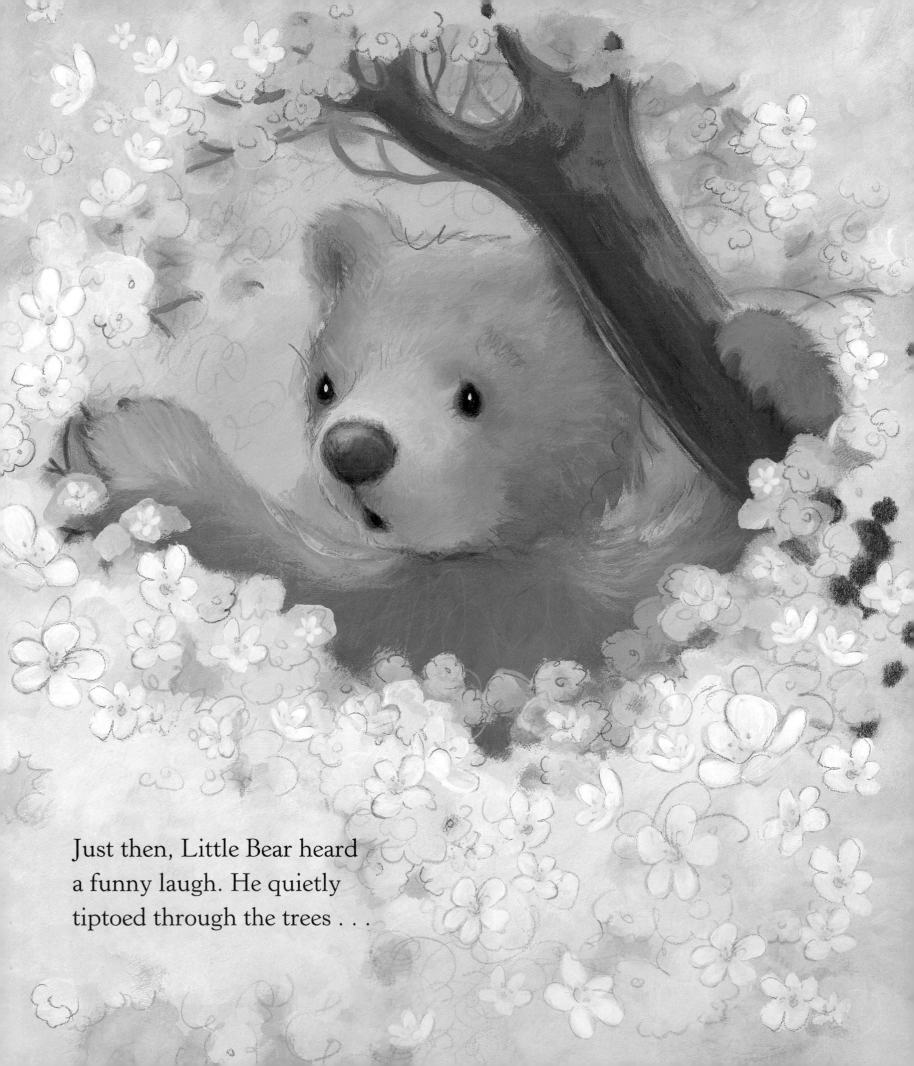

Just then, Little Bear heard
a funny laugh. He quietly
tiptoed through the trees . . .

There was Squirrel, dressed as a snowman!

"We've missed you, Bear," squealed Mole.

"Hide-and-seek isn't the same without you!"

Little Bear's eyes lit up. He had everything
he could wish for right in front of him – the
best friends in all the world.